THE CAROL MORAN

THE
CAROL

THE MACMILLAN COMPANY

NEW YORK

MORAN

WRITTEN AND ILLUSTRATED BY

PETER BURCHARD

U. S. 1025532

NOTE

The *Carol Moran* is a real tug, Chip is a real boy, and of course the *Queen Mary* is a real ocean liner, but the other characters in this book are make-believe.

The author would like to thank the members of the Moran Towing and Transportation Co., Inc. who helped make this book possible.

THE CAROL MORAN

Chip and his grandfather stood at the end of the pier and looked out at the busy river. The morning sun made flecks of gold on the water.

[9]

"There's the *Carol Moran*," said Chip's grandfather, pointing toward the middle of the river. As the tug came toward
them, she seemed to be just what Chip had expected, a little

boat with a big shaggy mane in front and other bumpers
on her sides. But as she pulled up to the pier, he saw that she
was much bigger than he had imagined a tug would be.

There was a big man standing in her bow. He threw a heavy looped line around one of the pilings.

"Hello Cap," he said.

"Hello Jim," said Chip's grandfather. "I'd like you to meet my grandson Chip. He's going along for the ride."

"That's fine," said Jim, smiling down at Chip. He reached out a big hand and helped Chip to the deck of the tug. Chip's grandfather jumped to the deck and went right up to the wheel-house and they moved out into the river.

"Do you know that this is your grandad's last trip?" asked Jim.

"Yes," said Chip, "he told me."

"We'll miss him," said Jim sadly.

Chip's grandfather had been telling him stories about tugs since he was old enough to listen, but this was Chip's first trip on one and he was too busy watching the river to feel sad. A ferry boat passed close to them. Other tugs went by and a

tanker steamed toward the ocean. They passed a railroad barge and Chip counted six boxcars on its deck. The tug that pulled them looked much older than the *Carol Moran* and had rubber tires hanging over her sides instead of rope bumpers.

Now they were passing one pier after another. As Chip looked toward shore he could see ships tied to most of them. One ship had stacks that were nearly as tall as the pier. She was being pushed toward the dock by two tugs at her bow and three more at her stern.

"That one is docking," said Jim. "It takes more tugs to dock a ship than to sail one."

Suddenly the *Carol Moran* slowed down and headed toward
one of the piers. Chip knew that tugs moved big ocean liners
and he wondered what kind of ship would be on the other side
of the pier. When they rounded the end of the pier Chip's heart
sank. There was no ship there at all. All he could see was three
old barges. The *Carol Moran* moved up to the barges and Jim
and another deck hand fastened her to the middle barge and

unhitched the lines that held the barges to the dock. Then the tug pulled the barges into the river. They passed two piers and pulled in and docked the barges behind an old tanker.

"Tugs do all kinds of jobs, don't they?" said Chip as he went over and stood near Jim.

"They do indeed. There's our next job," he said, pointing down the river. "We're going to dock that freighter."

As they moved toward the freighter another tug steamed toward her too. They drew close to the freighter and Chip could see a man leaning over the side grinning down at them through his black beard. The name *Rio Rose* was painted high on the ship's rusty stern.

"She doesn't look much like a rose, does she?" said Jim.

The two tugs eased the old freighter into her place at one of the empty piers.

"That ship came from Brazil," said Jim, "and she's probably loaded with coffee. Speaking of coffee, as soon as I've made us fast to the end of that pier we can have some lunch."

Chip was hungry and he was glad to go to the galley with Jim. The galley was warm and smelled of stew and fresh coffee. The cook was a short, round man. He was wearing a little round hat that looked like a cake with white frosting on it.

"Manuel, I'd like you to meet Chip," said Jim. "Chip is Cap's grandson."

"Happy to meet you," Manuel said.

They sat down at the table. Chip thought that Manuel must be the busiest man on the tug. He didn't stop moving for a minute. He stirred the stew with a big wooden spoon and tasted it and shook a little more pepper into it. He opened the oven to look at a pie. Every few minutes he ran a wet rag over the counter.

Chip's grandfather came in and sat down at one end of the table and some of the other men came in too. There wasn't room at the table for everyone and some of the men stood in the doorway.

"Don't tell me you're all hungry at once," said Chip's grandfather, looking a little puzzled.

Jim got to his feet. "Cap," he said, "I'm not much good at making speeches but we all wanted you to know how much we're going to miss you so we got you a little present." Jim took a brightly wrapped package out of his shirt pocket and gave it to the captain who unwrapped the box, opened it and took out a brand new wrist watch.

"My," he said. "She's a beauty." He turned the watch over and smiled when he saw the words, FROM THE MEN OF THE CAROL MORAN, on the back. "This is the nicest thing you could have given me," he said.

"Are we going to move any big ships today?" Chip asked as they finished lunch.

The Captain's eyes twinkled. "A tug can't do exciting work all the time," he said. "Tugs are the workhorses of the harbor. They go where they're told to go and do what they're told to do, but there's always a chance that there's a surprise ahead."

Chip followed Jim out to the deck and his grandfather went to the wheelhouse. The *Carol Moran* started up the river and for the first time she moved fast. Chip held tight to the shaggy bumper at the bow and looked straight ahead as the water was churned to a high white foam and swirled away behind them. Finally they slowed down. Jim came up and stood in the bow. Chip looked toward shore and suddenly he saw three big smokestacks towering above one of the piers. "Wow!" he said. "That's a big one."

"That's the *Queen Mary*," said Jim.

"Are we going to help her sail?" Chip asked, his eyes nearly as big as silver dollars.

"We are," said Jim with a broad grin, "and the best of it is that we're going to do it alone."

The *Queen Mary* was white on top and her hull was black.

As Chip looked up he felt the way he felt at parades when the excitement was almost more than he could stand.

A little girl stood at the rail high above them. She leaned over and waved at Chip and he waved back. The *Carol Moran* moved along the side of the *Queen Mary*. Gently she pushed her shaggy bow against the bow of the *Queen Mary*.

Chip looked straight up and saw a man leaning over the *Queen Mary*'s rail. The man signaled to Jim and threw a light line to him. As it came down it looked like a giant scribble. Jim caught it and tied it to a heavy towline and the men on the *Queen Mary* pulled it up and over her side. Then the *Carol Moran* moved away until the towline was tight so that she could hold the *Queen*'s bow away from the pier.

"You'd better go back to the stern," said Jim. "If this line snapped it would make you into mincemeat."

Chip went to the stern. The *Queen*'s whistle blew a long, loud blast. As they moved toward the middle of the river Chip could hear a band playing.

The *Queen Mary* stood like a giant whale over the *Carol Moran*. For half a minute Chip imagined that she really was a whale and would swallow their tug in one great gulp.

The pier soon looked small and far away but the people at the end of it were still waving. Their handkerchiefs flickered like little white birds in the afternoon sun.

When the *Carol Moran* had pushed the *Queen* around until she was pointing straight down the river, a man lowered the towline back to the tug. Some of the people on the *Queen* threw confetti and long red, yellow and blue streamers down toward the deck of the tug.

They sailed along beside the *Queen Mary* which was sliding slowly ahead of them.

Chip saw an opening in her great black side. They pulled alongside the *Queen* and Jim put a ladder up and held it while a man climbed across from the opening to the top deck of the tug. When the man was safely on board, Jim came over to where Chip was standing. "That was the docking pilot," he said. "He stays with the big ships until they are safely in the middle of the river."

The *Queen* traveled faster and faster and the *Carol Moran*
dropped behind. Chip ran up to the top deck and watched the
Queen steam off down the river. She was long and slim and
graceful. The seagulls wheeled slowly after her as she grew

smaller and smaller. Jim had been watching the *Queen Mary* too. "I bet you'd like to be sailing with her," he said.

"I would," said Chip, "but I'm glad to be on the *Carol Moran.*"

[39]

The tug moved back down the river to her own pier. The Captain came down from the wheelhouse and shook hands with Jim.

"Come back and see us, Cap," said Jim, "and bring Chip along."

Chip and his grandfather walked along the pier and then across the park. The Captain was very quiet.

"Maybe I'll be a tugboat man when I grow up," said Chip.

Then his grandfather smiled broadly for the first time all day. "Now maybe you will," he said.